READY, SET, SWIM!

TEXT BY GAIL DONOVAN
ILLUSTRATIONS BY DAVID AUSTIN CLAR STUDIO

Night Sky Books
New York • London

It was early morning in Miss Octavia Cuttle's school for fish.

"Attention, class," called Miss Cuttle. "While Pearl, Tug, and Little Blue finish their project, the rest of you may play outside."

"Early recess!" cheered Rainbow Fish and his friends as they jetted out of the cave.

"Let's have our own sports day," suggested Rosie.
"We can have races."

Spike whined, "That's no fun. You always win."

"Don't be a poor sport before we even get started,"
said Rainbow Fish. "We can split into teams."

"That's a great idea! I'll be the judge," said Dyna. "Rainbow Fish, Rosie, and Puffer, you can be on one team; Spike, Angel, and Rusty will be on the other."

Puffer whispered to Rosie, "They don't stand a chance with slowpoke Rusty on their team."

Dyna overheard him. "Don't be so sure," she said. "We're going to have all kinds of races."

"Let the games begin!" Dyna cried. "Rosie and Spike, you're up first in a race to the finish line. Ready, set, go!"

Rosie got off to a fast start and pulled ahead quickly. Spike gave up before Rosie even crossed the finish line.

"That was my best race ever." Rosie whooped. "I beat you by a mile, Spike."

"Don't exaggerate. You sound like Puffer," Angel told her.

"Not fair!" yelled Spike. "I wasn't ready! Rosie got a head start! Do over!"

"But, Spike, you gave up," said Rainbow Fish. "You didn't even finish the race."

"Our daredevil divers, Puffer and Angel, are up next," called Dyna.

"Angel doesn't stand a chance," bragged Puffer. "I've won every competition I've ever entered."

"Oh, Puffer, there you go again!" Angel cried.

"You're up first, Angel," Dyna quickly chimed in.
Angel's dive was a classic, swirly somersault.

"Puffer, you're up next," announced Dyna.

Puffer zigged and zagged, he flipped and flopped, he puffed in and out as he dived.

"Incredible!" said Dyna. "Puffer wins for originality."

"Told you so!" Puffer gloated.

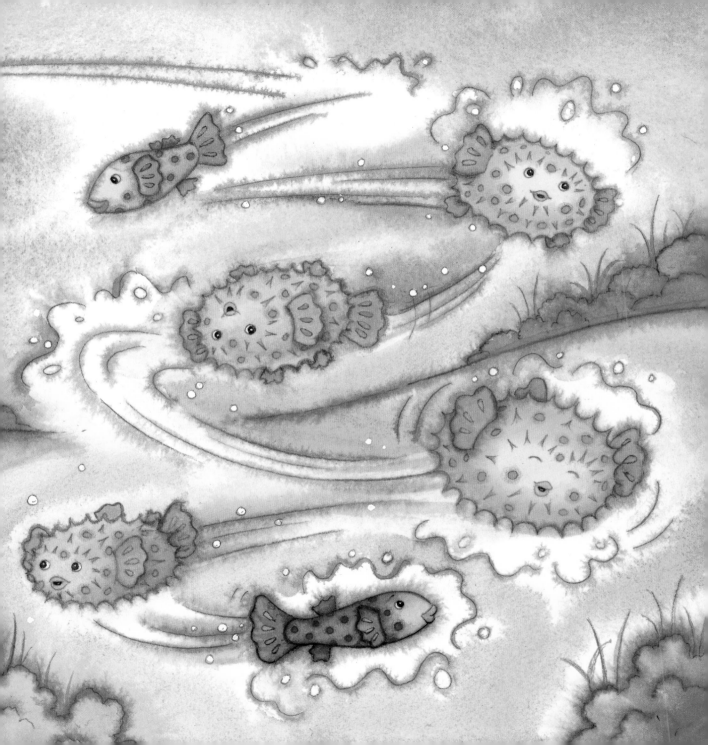

"O-o-o-oh, that's not fair!" complained Angel. "I learned my dive at water-ballet school in the Western Waters. Puffer didn't do a real dive, he just made one up."

"I knew we'd lose that round. Your dive wasn't exciting enough," said Spike.

"At least she tried," said Rosie. "She didn't give up—like some fish we know."

"On with the games," said Dyna. "Rainbow Fish and Rusty, you haven't gone yet."

"This isn't fun anymore. I don't want to play," said Rainbow Fish.

"Me neither," said Rusty. "I'm afraid we'll end up fighting, just like everyone else."

Rosie looked embarrassed. "I guess we can't have a good sports day if we're bad sports," she said.

"So what do we do?" asked Spike.

Dyna's tail lit up. "I have an idea," she said. "Follow me."

Dyna led the teams down into the depths of the sunken ship. "Let's have a relay race," she said. "Only this time, it's not just about speed or strength or originality. Everyone on the team has to work together! The last part of the relay is an obstacle course—Rainbow Fish against Rusty. And remember, you can't knock anything over!"

The teams were tied, coming into the last part of the race. But Rainbow Fish flashed through the obstacles while Rusty swam carefully along. As Rainbow Fish looped-the-loop, he knocked over two piles of shells. So even though Rainbow Fish crossed the finish line first, Rusty won. He hadn't disturbed a single shell or rock.

"Good race, Rusty!" called Rainbow Fish.

"I knew you could do it, Rusty!" shouted Spike.

"I guess slow and steady sometimes wins the race," said Puffer.

"Looks like our sports day turned out all right," said Rosie.

"Thanks to some good sports."